Dunlap

Tricycle Press
P.O. Box 7123
Berkeley, California 94707
www.tenspeed.com

Library of Congress Cataloging-in-Publication Data

Winton, Tim.
The deep / Tim Winton; illustrated by Karen Louise.
p. cm.
Summary: Alice overcomes her fear of deep water
when playful dolphins visit her family's beach.
ISBN 1-58246-024-8
[1. Fear–Fiction. 2. Swimming–Fiction. 3. Dolphins–Fiction.]
I. Louise, Karen, ill. II. Title.
PZ7.W7683 Dg 2000
[E]–dc21   99-055484

First published in 1998 by Sandcastle Books
First Tricycle Press printing, 2000
This edition has been modified for American readers.

Printed in Singapore

1 2 3 4 5 6 – 04 03 02 01 00

The Deep

Tim Winton

Illustrated by Karen Louise

Tricycle Press

Alice lived by the sea. She played every day in the sand
dunes and on the beach near her house. Even though
she was the youngest in her family, she wasn't
scared of many things. Snakes and spiders didn't
bother her. She wasn't scared of the dark. She
didn't worry much about thunder and lightning.

But, she was afraid of the deep.

Every morning Alice's family went down to the jetty for a swim.
Her mom dived in and scooted along like a torpedo.
Her dad made huge bellyflops that wet everyone, even the
seagulls in the air.

Jesse liked doing tin soldiers. He went in straight as a stick with no splash. Harry did cannonballs off the top rail – kabooom! Everyone sputtered and splashed and laughed in the smooth dark water.

But, Alice watched from the jetty. The water looked beautiful. It went all greeny-blue out there. It was deep. So deep you couldn't see the bottom.

Every day, Harry called to her, "Come on, Alice!
It's great! Jump in!"
It did look fun. They looked like dolphins,
her family, and she wanted to be one of
them. But, she was scared
of the deep.

Some mornings Alice
lay on the jetty to watch
the real dolphins swim
by. She stretched an arm
through the big smooth
planks to touch them, but she
couldn't reach. She saw schools
of whitebait racing out from the
shallows. She watched jellyfish
float by, hardly moving at all. She
picked mussels from the piles and
saved them for lunch. She hung around
on the jetty doing lots of things. But,
she didn't jump into the deep.

Alice wished she could be a seagull so she could
fly out over the deep and see forever.

"Swimming's like flying," said Harry. "Watch this!"

He pulled on his mask and snorkel and glided down through the water, rising and turning in the current like a gull on the wind.

Alice could see what he meant. She wished she could be like him. But, he was older.

Sometimes, Alice let her dad piggyback her out of the shallows and into the deep. He was like a big old horse swimming under her. She held on tight to his hair and was only a tiny bit afraid.

"Come on, Alice!" everyone called. "You can do it. Let go. Just pretend you're in the shallows."

Alice wanted to, but she couldn't. She didn't want to be scared of anything. Being frightened of the deep made her miserable.

Sometimes, Alice got sick of being frightened. She dog paddled around in the shallows for a while. Then, she took a big breath and headed out to where the others were diving and splashing.

She tried to be brave when the water began to change from green to blue. But, she turned back every time. She waded to the beach and sat down and cried. She turned her back so no one would see.

She hated being small. Being stuck in the shallows. She could swim, couldn't she? So why couldn't she swim in the deep?

One morning while Alice was on the beach digging, the dolphins came right into the warm shallows chasing whitebait and bony herring. The little fish made fountains as they leapt into the air, trying to escape. Some even bounced off Alice before falling back into the water.

Alice threw down her shovel and waded towards the dolphins.

One of them slapped the water with its tail. Alice dived in after it and chased it under water a little way. Other dolphins wheeled and swerved around her.

She pushed her head clear of the water and paddled after them as fast as she could. Each time she got close, giggling and panting, the dolphins surged away.

The water got bluer and bluer. The dolphins dived and leapt together into the air. Alice laughed. The water was like a silk sheet around her. It was the most wonderful feeling in thc world.

Then, something bumped against her. It wasn't a dolphin – it was Harry! He popped up beside her, spouting from his snorkel.

"Told you it was easy!" he said, sounding like he had a clothespin on his nose.

"What?" said Alice. "What's easy?"

"The deep. You're swimming in the deep!"

Alice went stiff. Suddenly, all she could think of was the great darkness below. She began to sink. Harry dived again and brought her sputtering back to the surface. Then, everyone was around her. She was in the deep. The deep!

"Swim!" they all yelled, laughing. "It's just water."

Alice got the giggles. She forgot about the dolphins. She didn't even think about what color the water was or how far down it went. She just kept going. Her arms and legs spun like wheels. They were right! It was just water. You could swim in the deep just as easily as in the shallows. She could.